Quinn

by Susan Hartley • illustrated by Anita DuFalla

Jim and Jen had Kit.

Ben had Mem.

Pam and Tam had the pup.

Pop had the tan cat.

Len had Quinn.

Sam and Dan put Tim

on the mat.

Quinn saw the pup.

He hit the pup.

Quinn went to Mem, the hen.

He hit the hen.

"Quit it, Quinn," said Len.

Quinn ran at the tan cat.
"Quinn! Quit it!" said Len.

Len put Quinn on the mat.

Quinn sat up on the mat.

Quinn did win!

Len said, "Good for you,
Quinn, but quit it."